MINTON

goes SAILING

ANNA FIENBERG
and
KIM GAMBLE

A
LITTLE
ARK
BOOK

ALLEN & UNWIN

Minton was a beachcombing salamander. He slept in a hammock under the stars and cooked his dinner on a barbecue.

'What'll it be tonight?' he asked himself, as he looked out at the darkening ocean. 'Hmm, my favourite snack, I think—crispy roasted worms with beetle sauce.'

Every morning Minton took his bucket and hurried down to the shore to see what the waves had washed up.

'The sea brings me everything I need,' he told his best friend, Turtle.

It was the sea that brought him the wood to make his toolbox. Inside he put his hammer and nails, scissors and glue, and anything else he might need.

Minton liked the beach life. And he loved to make things. But he also wanted to explore.

'Who do you think lives on that island over there?' Minton asked Turtle one day.

'A monster that eats rocks? No one I'd like to meet, that's for sure,' said Turtle.

'Well,' said Minton, 'one day I will sail over and see. I am going to make a boat, and travel the world.'

'You'd better make anti-monster armour then, too,' snorted Turtle.

Minton had to wait almost a week before the sea brought him the first thing he needed.

'Bingo!' he cried. 'Here is the hull of my boat.' He opened his toolbox and took out his paints.

'It'll never float,' said Turtle. 'You'll sink like a rock and the monster will get you.'

'Bingo!' Here is the mast of my boat.'
Minton opened his toolbox and pulled out a
piece of cork.

'It'll break,' said Turtle. 'First wave that comes
along. You'll be somebody's breakfast.'

'Bingo! Here is my sail.' Minton took some string from his toolbox.

'Yuk!' said Turtle. 'Who knows what's been in that bag? Old fish bones and slimy sandwiches, I bet.'

Minton finished making his boat at sunset. That night, after his dinner of centipede stew, he laid out all the things he would need on his journey. He packed his towel, his torch, his life-jacket and toolbox neatly into the boat, ready for the morning. He was so excited he wriggled and jiggled in his hammock. Then he lay awake looking at the stars, wondering if they would look different when he was on the island.

'You're not really going, are you?' asked Turtle.

'I certainly am,' said Minton. 'Are you coming?'

Turtle sighed. 'I suppose I'd better. After all, *I* wear anti-monster armour on my back. You'll see, I'll come dashing to save you, as usual.'

Minton sang as they cruised along. Seagulls flapped above, little waves licked gently at the boat below.

'This is the only way to travel, eh, Turtle?' said Minton.

Suddenly the sail ballooned with a fresh breeze and the boat began to zip along, scudding over the waves.

'We'll have to turn about if we're ever going to set foot on land again,' said Turtle.

But as they were turning, a blast of wind tipped them right over, and Minton and Turtle fell into the sea.

'Keep your eyes open for monsters!' Turtle managed to shout before they sank under the waves. A long dark shape flashed past, like a black arrow.

Minton and Turtle swam fast underwater, popping up to the surface like corks. They saw the boat lying on its side.

'Take the anchor rope, Turtle,' said Minton. 'There's only one thing for it—you'll have to tow us to the island.'

Turtle took the rope in his mouth and began a slow, told-you-so stroke with his flippers.

When they arrived at the island, Minton and Turtle pulled the boat up onto the sand.

They plunged into the jungle, Minton hacking at the vines with his saw.

Turtle took a deep breath. 'Perfume!' he said. 'These flowers smell good enough to eat.'

Minton popped a golden berry into his mouth. Honey spilled over his tongue. 'Delicious! This is a treasure island.'

Turtle watched Minton carefully to make sure the golden berries weren't poisonous. Then he helped pick a pile and they sat down to eat their lunch.

Suddenly there was a loud *thump thump* close by. 'The rock-eating monster!' cried Turtle.

Leaves crunched and a bush behind them shook.
Something groaned. Minton jumped with fright.

The branches were pushed apart and a face
peeped out.

'Sizzling somersaults! I'm glad to see you two.'

A tiny girl stepped toward them with her hand outstretched. 'I'm Bouncer the acrobat,' she said, 'and I'm tired of talking to plants.'

'Hello,' said Minton. 'What is an acrobat doing on this island?'

'Trying to bounce again,' she replied.

Bouncer did a cartwheel, landing neatly at Turtle's feet.

'I used to work in a circus, very far away. I could do the highest jumps. But one day I couldn't stop. I did such a high jump, such a gigantic, enormous jump, that I flew over the city, over the farms and valleys, over the sea until I landed—plop!—right here on this island. And now I have no bounce left at all.'

'But don't you like it here?' asked Minton. 'You can eat these honeypot berries, and Turtle and I can visit you in our boat.'

Bouncer sighed. 'I miss the circus. I miss all my cousins and brothers and sisters and friends who live there. And I won't see them ever again!'

Minton stroked Bouncer's hand.

'I've never been to the circus,' he said softly. He looked out at the horizon, thinking. 'It would probably take too long to go to the other side of the world in my boat. I suppose we'll just have to build an aeroplane.'

'Cadoodling cartwheels!' cheered Bouncer. 'When do we start?'

'It'll never work,' said Turtle. 'You'll drop like a stone into the sea and the killer whales will eat you.'

But Minton was already hurrying down to the
shore to see what the sea would bring.

To make Minton's boat you'll need: a margarine or butter tub, 3 bamboo skewers, 2 corks, string, a plastic bag, scissors or sharp knife, tape or glue, and paint.

1. Trim tub to shape, and paint

2. Cut cork

3. Assemble mast (note, lower spar is longer than top spar)

The more weight in your boat the better it will sail.

4. Attach mast to boat, sprit at front goes into bottom cork. Secure with string. Cut sail to size and attach